Wild Violet!

Written by Alex Latimer
Illustrated by Patrick Latimer

For Eva and Olivia - P.L.

Lancashire Library Services	
30118136932062	
PETERS	JF
£6.99	31-Jul-2018
NLA	

First published in the United Kingdom in 2018 by
Pavilion Children's Books
43 Great Ormond Street
London
WC1N 3HZ

An imprint of Pavilion Books Limited.

Publisher and Editor: Neil Dunnicliffe
Assistant Editor: Harriet Grylls
Art Director: Anna Lubecka

Text © Alex Latimer 2018

Illustrations © Patrick Latimer 2018

The moral rights of the author and illustrator have been asserted

ISBN: 9781843653820

A CIP catalogue record for this book is available from the British Library.

10 9 8 7 6 5 4 3 2 1

Reproduction by ColourDepth, UK

Printed in China by 1010 Printing International Limited

This book can be ordered directly from the publisher online at www.pavilionbooks.com,
or try your local bookshop.

Violet was born wild.

"It won't last long," people said. "She'll be good as gold by the time she turns three."

But Violet turned three.

Then she turned four.

And she was
as wild as ever.

She refused to wash.

Her face was always
dirty and her hair
was filled with
bits of food and twigs
from climbing trees.

She ate her dinner with her hands

and slurped her cereal
straight from the bowl.

She growled at the dog
and drew on the walls
and stayed up all night shrieking.

Her parents
were exhausted.
So they called Violet's
grandmother and begged
her to take Violet for
one afternoon.

"We just want to take
a nap," they cried.

Violet's gran thought
that a visit to the zoo
would do her good.

"The fresh air is calming," she said, "and sometimes I like to sit and watch the birds in the duck pond."

But the zoo animals
just showed Violet how
to be even wilder.

The last enclosure they visited was the Monkey House and by then gran was exhausted too.

In fact, she was so exhausted
that when she reached for Violet's
hand to take her home, she took
the hand of a monkey instead!

And worst of all,

gran didn't notice!

When gran buckled Violet into the car,
Violet wriggled and kicked.
It wasn't unusual.

And while gran drove home, Violet scratched
at the upholstery. Just like she always did.

And when she dropped
Violet with her parents,
she yelled and shrieked.
Typical Violet.

But here is the wildest
part of this story:

Violet's parents didn't notice either!

The monkey had bits of food and twigs in his hair.

He ate his lunch with his hands.

He growled at the dog and
drew on the walls and
shrieked all afternoon.

So Violet's parents bathed him and fed
him and put him to bed.

Back at the zoo,
Violet was having a
wonderful time too.
She loved living
with the monkeys;
they shrieked and
kicked and bit
and climbed.

They threw litter at each other and dribbled water out of their mouths. They drew with mud on the walls and they ate their food with their feet.

"This is great," said Violet. "I'll stay here forever!"

But that night Violet couldn't sleep.
No one had tidied up all the mess
she had made or mopped up the
water she had splashed.

The hay was cold and damp
and none of the monkeys knew
how to read her a bedtime story
or tuck her in.

In the morning there was no warm bath
or tasty breakfast. Or a hug and a kiss
from mum and dad.
She began to miss her home and her parents.

Of course, it didn't take the
zoo people long to notice that
something was wrong.

The zoo keeper phoned
Violet's mum and dad.
"You daughter is living in our monkey enclosure -
I think you must have one of our monkeys."

Violet's mum and dad
were shocked and
embarrassed.

They buckled the monkey into the
car and raced down to the zoo.

And do you know what they found
in the monkey cage?

They found a girl with neatly brushed hair and a face washed clean.

A girl who didn't screech or hit or kick or bite.

"Mum, dad - I missed you! I don't like being wild
and I don't like being dirty. I want to go home
and have a bath and eat with a fork
and sleep in my own warm bed."

And so they said goodbye to the monkey - who had missed his own mum and dad too - and they drove home.

Violet didn't bite or
scratch in the car.
She didn't growl at the
dog or draw on the walls
or shriek all night long.

She was very well
behaved from then on.

But some days - and you mustn't tell anyone -
Violet's mum takes her to the zoo, and she has
a playdate with the monkeys.

Because even though she behaves
and listens to her parents and does all
of her school work - she's still quite
wild inside, and that's okay.